SUPERMAN
RETURNS ™

Earthquake in Metropolis!
by David E. Sky

Superman created by Jerry Siegel and Joe Shuster.

First edition. Printed and manufactured in China.
All rights reserved.
ISBN: 0-696-22909-9

We welcome your comments and suggestions. Write to us
at: Meredith Books, Children's Books,
1716 Locust St., Des Moines, IA 50309-3023.
meredithbooks.com

Lex Luthor, Superman's greatest enemy, and his evil band of criminals made their way through deep snow. They were looking for Superman's secret hiding place in the Arctic, the Fortress of Solitude.

As soon as they reached the Fortress, Lex stepped forward. "Now to find the crystal Superman's father gave him. I can use it to create an earthquake like Metropolis has never seen before!" Lex said, with an icy smile.

Lex stood in the bright white Fortress made entirely of crystals and looked at the single crystal in his hand. "Let's see Superman save Metropolis now," he said.

Clark Kent was ready to have a great morning! With a smile on his face, he walked into the Daily Planet building. Clark worked as a reporter for the great paper covering the city of Metropolis.

Clark's friend, Lois Lane, was the paper's star reporter. She always covered the top stories, but so far it was a slow news day in Metropolis.

"Hi, Mr. Kent!" Jimmy Olsen said, when he saw Clark come in. Jimmy was a photographer for the paper.

"Hey, Jimmy," said Clark.

"There's not much happening in the news today," Jimmy told Clark. "The city is quiet, for a change."

Then, Perry White, the editor in chief of the newspaper, opened the door to his office and announced, "Everyone! Staff meeting in five minutes!"

Meanwhile, in his secret hideout
Lex was plotting something
extremely dangerous.

Lex and his gang were looking at a model of the city of Metropolis.

Lex had created a perfect version of Metropolis in miniature, complete with a working train.

Lex also had the crystal he had stolen from Superman's Fortress of Solitude. Holding it up, he declared, "Now to test the powers of this crystal. This will give me the ability to destroy Metropolis."

Kitty Kowalski, Lex's girlfriend, said, "But I don't understand, Lex. Why would you want to destroy Metropolis? Lots of people live here. Won't they be in danger?"

"They don't matter," Lex told Kitty. "I want to know what this crystal can do. As for Metropolis, who cares? Maybe Superman will save the city. It's not my problem."

Back at the *Daily Planet*, Perry White was telling the staff of the paper, "We need to find some breaking news stories! Where is Superman? He's always good for a headline."

Clark Kent tried not to look nervous. No one at the paper knew that he actually was Superman.

Jimmy was checking his camera when he felt the building begin to shake. "What was that?" he asked.

The building shook again, and Lois crouched on the ground, worried. "I don't know," she said. "Where is Clark?"

Clark had run down to the street to find out what was going on. Because he was Superman, he could tell before anyone else that something was wrong.

As he felt the ground rumble again,
Clark knew the shaking was about
to get worse. He ran back to
the *Daily Planet*.

Suddenly the ground was shaking
uncontrollably. It was an earthquake!
People began running into the streets
in panic.

Up in the *Daily Planet* newsroom, everyone ran to escape as the building began to tremble. No one noticed that Clark had sneaked into a nearby closet.

Clark emerged from the closet after everyone had gone. He had changed into Superman.

Frightened, Jimmy ran out of the
Daily Planet building to look for cover.
People in the streets ran as parts of the
buildings fell from above.

Also on the street, Perry White said, "When I asked for headlines, I didn't mean this!" Like Jimmy, he was also scared, although he was trying not to show it.

"Look," someone called out. "Superman is up there!" Sure enough, Superman was on top of the Daily Planet building.

Superman raced through Metropolis, rescuing people and repairing earthquake damage. He even caught the globe from the Daily Planet building as it plummeted toward the frightened crowds on the street below.

"Ooh, that Superman!" Lex declared to his gang at the secret hideout. "I will get him one of these days."

"Congratulations, Superman," Perry said. "You've saved the city again. Looks like the *Daily Planet* has its headline for tomorrow!"

"I'm happy to help," Superman said, just before soaring into the sky.

At the end of the day, Lois and Clark left the *Daily Planet* together.

"Superman sure is amazing," Lois said. Clark just smiled.